TINTIN AND THE PICAROS

Ah! there you are . . . Come on in. I want you to read something. Look what I found in the latest "Paris-Flash" . . .

"Opera star Bianca Castafiore continues her brilliant progress through South America. After triumphs in Ecuador, Colombia and Venezuela, she visits San Theodoros, where she will be received by General Tapioca."

General Tapioca . . . Didn't he topple our old friend Alcazar?

Yes, with the help of the Kûrvi-Tasch regime in Borduria. They say Tapioca's a real tyrant . . . he's cruel and he's vain . . .

. . . In fact he's so vain he changed the name of the capital from Los Dopicos. He called it Tapiocapolis after himself. As for poor old Alcazar, he's gone underground with a band of partisans.

Oh, yes: the famous Picaros.

That's right, the Picaros. It's the name adopted by the guerrillas who've sworn to get rid of Tapioca and his mob. They're said to be backed by another great power . . . commercial and financial this time: the International Banana Company . . . A rare old mix-up, as you see!

Blistering barnacles, Tintin! What a lecture! . . . All that talking makes me thirsty . . . Here, have a whisky . . .

No, thanks. Not for me . . . You know that.

Oh well . . . Cheers!

PFOUAGH!

HERGÉ
★
THE ADVENTURES OF
TINTIN
★

TINTIN
AND THE
PICAROS

EGMONT

The TINTIN books are published in the following languages:

Afrikaans	HUMAN & ROUSSEAU
Armenian	SIGEST
Bengali	ANANDA PUBLISHERS PVT, LTD
Brazilian Portuguese	COMPANHIA DAS LETRAS
Catalan	JUVENTUT
Chinese complex (HK)	CASTERMAN / THE COMMERCIAL PRESS (HK) LTD
Chinese Complex (TW)	COMMONWEALTH MAGAZINES
Chinese simplified	CASTERMAN / CHINA CHILDREN PRESS & PUBLICATION GROUP
Croatian	ALGORITAM
Creole (Gouad. & Martin)	CARAÏBEDITIONS
Creole (Réun & Mauric)	EPSILON EDITIONS
Czech	ALBATROS
Danish	COBOLT
Dutch	CASTERMAN
Finnish	OTAVA
French	CASTERMAN
English (US)	HACHETTE BOOKS (LITTLE, BROWN & CO)
English (UK)	EGMONT UK LTD
Estonian	TÄNAPÄEV
Georgian	AGORA EDITIONS
German	CARLSEN VERLAG
Greek	MAMOUTH COMIX
Hindi	OM BOOKS
Hungarian	EGMONT
Indonesian	PT GRAMEDIA
Italian	LIZARD EDIZIONI
Icelandic	FORLAGID
Japanese	FUKUINKAN SHOTEN
Khmer	CASTERMAN
Korean	CASTERMAN / SOL PUBLISHING
Latvian	ZVAIGZNE ABC PUBLISHERS
Lithuanian	ALMA LITTERA
Mongolian	CASTERMAN
Norwegian	EGMONT
Polish	EGMONT
Portuguese	ASA EDITORIAL
Russian	CASTERMAN
Romanian	M.M.EUROP
Slovenian	UCILA
Spanish (castellano)	JUVENTUD
Swedish	BONNIER CARLSEN
Thai	NATION EGMONT
Turkish	INKILAP
Tibetan	CASTERMAN
Welsh	DALEN

TRANSLATED BY
LESLIE LONSDALE-COOPER AND MICHAEL TURNER

EGMONT
We bring stories to life

Artwork copyright © 1976 by Editions Casterman, Paris and Tournai.
Copyright © renewed 1973 by Casterman.
Text copyright © 1976 by Egmont UK Limited.
First published in Great Britain in 1976 by Methuen Children's Books.
This edition published in 2012 by Egmont UK Limited,
The Yellow Building, 1 Nicholas Road, London W11 4AN.

Library of Congress Catalogue Card Numbers Afor 83870
ISBN 978 1 4052 0635 8

37271/40

Printed in China
13 15 17 19 20 18 16 14

RRRRING

RRRRING

Hello? . . . Yes . . . WHO?

Jolyon Wagg, yes! . . . Hi! . . . Now look here, I just saw old Castanette on the telly . . . And what do I hear? Blow me if she hasn't got her knick-knacks insured now . . .

. . . and for a pretty penny too! . . . Strikes me you could have pushed the business my way . . . for old Rock Bottom insurance! What's the use of having friends, I say to myself, if they let you down at the first opportunity? . . . Come on, when you want to do someone a good turn, there's always a way! . . . Yes, I do! . . . And I don't mind saying so! . . . And while I'm on . . .

What? . . . But I . . . How . . . Well I'm . . . But . . . Excuse me . . . Look here . . .

Well I'll be . . . !! That's beyond a joke!

SLAM

In fact it's the thundering limit! . . . I'm taken to task by that weevil Wagg because he wasn't asked to insure Castafiore's jewellery!

PFOUAGH!

Billions of bilious blue blistering barnacles! . . . PFFF! . . . It's poi   -son!

POISON ???

Nonsense, Captain! Who on earth would want to poison you? I know you've got a few enemies, but not as deadly as that.

Maybe . . . Anyway, I don't feel at all well.

Something wrong with this whisky? It tastes pretty good to me!

Have a lie down, Captain. It'll go . . .

Good night! You'll feel better in the morning.

All the same, I wonder . . .

SNOWY!

Snowy, you're hopeless! You've drunk all that spilt whisky!

Showhat? . . . Wassa matter? Wassamatter with a drop of whisky?

HIC

Still, it certainly proves the whisky isn't poisoned.

Come on, off to bed, you old dipso! Sleep off the booze!

HIC

Next morning . . .

I look horrible this morning . . . Must have been that wretched whisky I had yesterday.

Oh well, too bad, can't be helped! . . . It's time for the news . . .

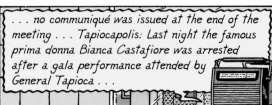

. . . no communiqué was issued at the end of the meeting . . . Tapiocapolis: Last night the famous prima donna Bianca Castafiore was arrested after a gala performance attended by General Tapioca . . .

. . . Statements by the authorities in San Theodoros have accused the star of plotting against the government . . .

Tintin! . . . Tintin! . . . Something marvellous just happened to General Tapioca!

He's arrested Castafiore, silly fellow! He doesn't know what he's let himself in for!

Arrested Castafiore? . . . No! . . .

He has you know: arrested her at the end of a concert . . . What a turn up, eh?

You could say so, yes . . .

Tintack! . . . Capock Hatpin! . . . Terrible news! . . . Dreadful!

Read this! In the "Daily Reporter"! Bianca Castafiore has been arrested!

Do they give any details?

That poor child! . . . In prison! . . . Just imagine! . . . I'm absolutely shattered!

GROOAHH!

Listen to this, Tintin: it's positively hilarious!

Go ahead, I'm all ears.

STAR IN TERRORIST PLOT
BIANCA CASTAFIORE ARRES

TAPIOCAPOLIS, T
International oper
Bianca (Milanese
Castafiore was a
tonight by the S
Theodoros pol
is accused of
against the st
Members of
entourage
taken into

"... A search of her luggage revealed documents which prove conclusively the existence of a plot aimed at the removal of General Tapioca and the overthrow of his regime ..."

... The San Theodorian government have let it be known that the plot is centred in a West European country, where the singer was staying before her departure for South America."

It's just like a cheap thriller!

Castafiore in a conspiracy! A conspiracy of silence, let's hope!!

DONG

Excuse me, sir, but there are two reporters downstairs ... asking if you will see them.

Already?!

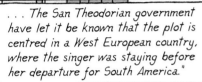
All right. Just let me put on a dressing-gown and I'll come.

Why, it's Christopher Willoughby-Drupe and Marco Rizotto of "Paris-Flash". What can I do for you, gentlemen?

Good-morning, Captain. Forgive us for calling so early, but we wanted to be the first to ask what you think of this Castafiore business.

What do I think? ... Perfectly simple! ...

I think it's a load of old rubbish! Blistering barnacles! Accusing Castafiore of conspiracy! ... Ridiculous!

Yes, but what about the accusations made against yourself?

Accusations against ME???

Ah, so you don't know about that yet? Here, look ... in today's "Trumpeter" ...

?

Impossible! . . . Those San Theodolites must be off their tripods!

Oh, it's you. Here, read this. It concerns you, too.

Me?

Yes, you! Read it! . . .

courageous action which will bring widespread benefits.

CASTAFIORE CONSPIRACY
TAPIOCA GOVERNMENT MAKES NEW CHARGES

Tapiocapolis: The Castafiore conspiracy was masterminded from Marlinspike in Western Europe, claimed a government spokesman today. He accused supporters of General Alcazar, and named as principal figures in the plot: Captain Haddock, Tintin the reporter, and Professor Cuthbert Calculus. All three are long-standing friends of General Alcazar. It is known that Signora Bianca Castafiore was recently a guest at Marlinspike Hall, country home of Captain

What is all this? They must be crazy!

You're telling me!

You deny it then?

I'll say we do! The whole story is bilge! Bilge from stem to stern!

DONG

?

'Morning squire!

"Daily Reporter"! Hi!

? !?

A few words for "Radio-Round", Captain . . .

. . . and for "Radio Rave-Up" . . .

Gentlemen, these accusations are as grotesque as they are false! Us? Conspirators? . . . Blue blistering bell-bottomed balderdash!

Seriously . . . Here comes Professor Calculus. Look at him, then tell me whether you think he's capable of taking part in a conspiracy!

?

Perfectly, my dear sirs! And proud of it!

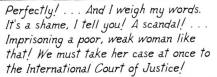

Perfectly! . . . And I weigh my words. It's a shame, I tell you! A scandal! . . . Imprisoning a poor, weak woman like that! We must take her case at once to the International Court of Justice!

You deny the allegations, Captain. All the same, General Alcazar is one of your friends, isn't he?

One of my friends? . . . I've met him two or three times, that's all.

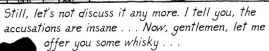

If you say so. But I take it you won't deny that Signora Castafiore has been a guest here, at your invitation? . . .

Invitation? You mean invasion! But from that to conspiracy . . .

Still, let's not discuss it any more. I tell you, the accusations are insane . . . Now, gentlemen, let me offer you some whisky . . .

Let's drink to the release of the Milanese Nightingale, and . . .

. . . your good health!

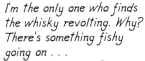

EURK!

Stop! Don't touch it! . . . There must be some mistake. This whisky is quite undrinkable!

Undrinkable? On the contrary, it's excellent!

Velvet!

Mmm . . .

You mustn't drink it, I tell you! It tastes like poison!

Of course, of course: a poison that kills slowly! It's a known fact! Ha! ha! ha!

And that's no problem: as it happens, we aren't in a hurry! Ha! ha! ha!

I'm the only one who finds the whisky revolting. Why? There's something fishy going on . . .

Unless . . . That's an idea . . . Maybe it's a new brand Nestor bought.

I must ask him . . .

I can't understand the master: I find this "Loch Lomond" superb, as always.

I say, Nestor . . .

Well, Nestor?

I . . . er . . . to tell the truth, sir, I was making sure it really is "Loch Lomond".

And your conclusion, my friend?

It is "Loch Lomond", sir. Indubitably!

I don't understand, not one little bit!

That evening . . .

What about having one more try?

No! Enough is enough! Don't let me hear any more about whisky!

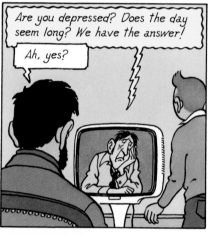

Are you depressed? Does the day seem long? We have the answer!

Ah, yes?

LOCH LOMOND

Impossible! They're doing it on purpose! It's a plot!

On the subject of plots . . . Listen!

. . . and to start our round-up, we bring you the latest on what is known as the Castafiore Conspiracy . . . with international reactions, and particularly those in San Theodoros. There, naturally, the response is particularly violent . . . as viewers worldwide were shown in this television interview with the San Theodorian president . . .

. . . General Tapioca, in Tapiocapolis. The general commented on what he called the "pantomime plotters".

. . . Let them tremble, I say! . . . Cowards, skulking in their dusty mansion . . .

. . . puppet-masters in this vile conspiracy! . . . Tremble, crooked Captain Haddock! . . . Tremble, treacherous Tintin and crafty Cuthbert Calculus!

Crafty yourself, you pachyrhizus! . . . And no one's more treacherous than you, you guano-gatherer!

I'll give him a piece of my mind all right, fancy-dress fascist! . . .

But . . .

Hello, International? . . . Give me South America . . . Tapiocapolis . . . General Tapioca! . . . What? . . . Tapioca, yes, as in tapioca . . . exactly!

I'm sorry, sir, but we don't stock tapioca. This is a butcher's shop, sir . . . Cutts the butcher! . . . Not at all, sir!

Thundering typhoons! Cutts again! Why do I always get him?

Why not send a telegram, anyway?

A telegram . . . You're right! . . . That's a very good idea: a telegram!

Wait, I'll give you the number . . .

And a few minutes later . . .

I'll repeat that: General Tapioca, Tapiocapolis, San Theodoros. Message reads: Profoundly shocked by false accusations made against us Stop We register formal and absolute denial Stop No regards Signed: Haddock, Tintin and Calculus.

Good! Thank you very much.

A greetings telegram, sir?

ARE YOU MAD?

Next morning . . .

Daily Reporter

HADDOCK: I DENY!

CAPTAIN FURIOUSLY DENIES PARTICIPATION IN ANY PLOT WHATSOEVER

TAPIOCA: I ACCUSE!

GENERAL CLAIMS IRREFUTABLE PROOF OF COLLUSION BETWEEN MARLINSPIKE CONSPIRATORS AND INTERNATIONAL BANANA COMPANY

General Tapioca, Tapiocapolis. Oh! You know that . . . Good. Message reads . . . er . . . Downright lies Stop Will make you swallow false allegations . . . Yes, in the plural . . . one day Stop You will end up hanging from yardarm. Yes, y as in yashmak . . . Stop.

Two days later . . .

Daily Reporter

TAPIOCA OFFERS HADDOCK ROUND TABLE TALKS IN TAPIOCAPOLIS

At a press conference today, General Tapioca announced that he is inviting Commodore Haddock and his companions to Tapiocapolis for a full, free, frank and fair exchange of views. Each visitor would receive a safe-conduct through the good offices of the embassy. "My only aim," asserted the General, "is to seek out the truth."

You know, he isn't a bad old stick really . . . I've a good mind to accept his invitation. That way, we'd show everyone our good faith.

Or else we'll find ourselves in prison, like Bianca Castafiore. Thanks very much!

Oh, you! Always suspicious! . . . Anyway, we've a safe-conduct.

I'm not in the least impressed, Captain. The safe-conduct could be nothing more than a decoy!

OOOH!

Have you seen? We've been invited there. We must go, Captain.

?

Yes, and find ourselves in prison like your precious Bianca! . . . That's plain as a pikestaff, my poor friend! . . . As for the safe-conduct, it's just a decoy!

Bravo! Well spoken! I'll pack my things and we'll go!

Next morning...

Daily Reporter

TALKS DRAMA
WILL HADDOCK & CO. RESPOND TO TAPIOCA INVITATION?

The following day...

Daily Reporter

HADDOCK SENSATION
NO!
I WON'T GO TO TAPIOCAPOLIS

And the day after . . .

Daily Reporter

HADDOCK BACKS DOWN
SAYS TAPIOCA: HE FEARS TRUTH

I'm backing down! . . . I'm afraid of the truth! All right, you dictatorial duckbilled diplodocus! I'll show you what sort of stuff I'm made of!

Calm down, Captain.

Calm down! Calm down! . . . I'm as cool as a cucumber!

He'd challenge me . . . that ostrogoth! All right, we shall see what we shall see!

Hello, Telegrams? . . . Yes . . . yes, naturally, for General Tapioca. Message reads . . .

Send safe-conducts (in the plural, safe-conducts) Stop Arriving by return of post . . . Signed: Haddock . . . Good. No! Ordinary rate!!!

The die is cast! . . . He'll find out what sort of fish he's hooked, that puffed-up Punchinello! . . . Tintin . . . we're going!

YOU may be going, Captain . . . I'm staying right here!!

??

What? What did you say?

I said I'm not going, Captain. You're quite free to fall into the trap they're trying to set for us, but as far as I'm concerned it's NIET!

Oh! You and your suspicions! They're an obsession! According to you, the world's composed of nothing but scallywags and scoundrels! . . . Why shouldn't General Tapioca be an honest sort of chap, eh? . . . Why? . . . Go on, tell me!

It's always possible, but . .

. . . I still think they're trying to entice us over there . . . I don't know the reason . . . but it positively reeks of trickery.

Ah! So that's it!

All right, stay here, Mister Mule! Stay tucked up, all safe and warm in your bedroom-slippers! Cuthbert and I are going out there to defend our honour, and yours too, against that thundering herd of Zapotecs! Finish!

Hm!

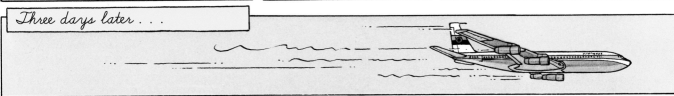

Three days later . . .

Ladies and gentlemen, in a few moments we shall be landing at Tapiocapolis. Please fasten your safety-belts and extinguish your cigarettes . . .

We're coming in to land, Professor.

Thailand? . . . Really? What a surprise . . .

⑪

D'you see? We're arriving in Tapiocapolis just in time for the famous carnival week . . .

In Greek??

"Taking part will be many performers from overseas including . . ." Why, look! There's a troupe from back home: The Jolly Follies!

Iced lollies? Now?

Aha! There's the reception committee . . .

Commodore Haddock?

Er . . . just captain . . . er . . .

Such modesty! Here, a man of your gallantry would be an admiral! . . . Allow me to present myself: Colonel Alvarez, aide-de-camp to His Excellency General Tapioca.

Delighted!

Professor Calculus, I presume? To you also, welcome to our country!

I'm sorry, officer, but I cannot shake a hand which grinds underfoot the imprescriptible rights of the human individual!

I . . . er . . . his little joke, of course! . . . Unfortunately, the Professor is still suffering from 'flu . . . as a result, the infection . . . er . . . you . . . you follow me?

So there!

Perfectly, Captain . . .

And this is our good friend Tintin, no doubt?

Welcome to San Theodoros, my young friend . . .

You're mistaken, Colonel! . . . It's like, man, we're the Dripping Tap . . . Like we're here for the carnival.

But then . . . Where is Tintin?

Well . . . er . . . I . . . He couldn't come . . . 'Flu . . . him too . . . Asian, of course . . . So, for fear of infection, you understand . . .

Yes, yes, I understand very well . . .

Won't you get in, gentlemen?

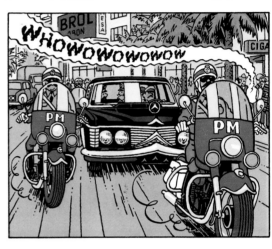

WHOWOWOWOWOW

Unfortunately, the General is unable to grant you an audience for two or three days. He has had to go on a tour of inspection in the north and he begs you to excuse him . . .

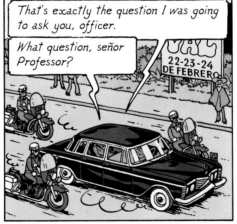

That's exactly the question I was going to ask you, officer.

What question, señor Professor?

That's no answer, soldier! I ask you, where is Signora Castafiore . . . Her spirit must be totally crushed, I'm sure, poor little thing . . .

On the contrary, dear Professor. I assure you, the morale of that charming lady is extremely high!

To Shanghai? . . . She's gone to Shanghai? . . . You dare to make fun of me?

No, no, Professor. I tell you she is delighted with her stay in San Theodoros . . .

. . . and next time, don't overcook my pasta!

He is devoted to you already; isn't that so, Manolo?

Good of you, Manolo! . . .

MMM!

He looks a thug!

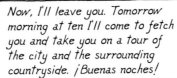

Now, I'll leave you. Tomorrow morning at ten I'll come to fetch you and take you on a tour of the city and the surrounding countryside. ¡Buenas noches!

Good night, Colonel.

¡Adios, Manolo! And remember your orders!

What a welcome, eh, Cuthbert my old shipmate! Come on, cheer up! Everything's going to be sorted out. Your beloved Bianca may be free tomorrow and we'll all have a good laugh!

A bath? . . . That's a good idea. I think I'll do the same.

These people are really charming! And Colonel Alvarez, so friendly, such style, so distinguished! . . .

Ministry of the Interior!

At once, Colonel!

And a few minutes later . . .

Good evening, Colonel. Is the Colonel in?

Colonel Esponja awaits you, Colonel!

Mission completed, Colonel. Everything is in order, and the circuits are live . . . However . . .

One moment, Colonel: let's check everything's working properly.

Yes, Colonel, but first of all I have to tell you . . .

Yes, yes, in a minute, Colonel, in a minute . . .

Ah! He's just found the bar!

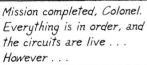

Oho! "Loch Lomond". These Tapiocans certainly do things in style!

SNIFF

PFOUAGH!

Hello, that doesn't seem to please him . . . Yet they assured us that was his favourite whisky.

Unbelievable! . . . It's still happening! . . . What's gone wrong? Why can't I take whisky any more?

Let's try something else . . . gin, for instance.

PFOUAGH!

He doesn't like that either? Just his bad luck! . . . Now for Channel No. 2 . . .

Colonel, I must tell you . . .

Ah, there he is! A pity he didn't agree to work for us . . . But who knows, he may change his mind some day . . .

Good. Now, Channel No. 3 . . .

Colonel, I must . . .

You must what, Colonel?

I must tell you . . . Number Three has not arrived, Colonel.

Not arrived?! . . . Szplug! Why not? . . . Where is he then?

He never left Europe, Colonel. Number One told me he had influenza and that . . .

And you tell me that now! . . . By the whiskers of Kûrvi-Tasch!!

Influenza! . . . So, he was suspicious! . . . But it's absolutely necessary for him to come! . . . And if I know him, he'll be coming anyway!

Good, I'll think about it. Meanwhile, you'll have to stall the others. Tell them everybody's got influenza . . . that the Castafiore's lost her voice . . . tell them anything you like . . . to gain time.

Very good, Colonel.

Meanwhile . . .

What a beautiful evening. It must be lovely outside . . .

Hello, what's this? Rusted up?

Come open . . . you stupid . . . stubborn . . .

CRACK

Billions of bilious blue blistering barnacles! Why does everything happen to me?!

¿Que pasa?

¿Que pasa? . . . Que pasa is that I tried to open that confounded window! . . . And kindly put away the blunderbuss: those things have a habit of going off!

No good to open, señor . . . air conditioning . . .

That may well be so, but I don't happen to like canned air. Kindly open the window, por favor!

Windows, they do not open, señor . . . Buenas noches, señor.

ZZING

Thanks, friend . . . really, you try too hard!

Have you quite finished chucking your guns out of the window?

?

Is this yours, eh?

Yes, is mine! . . . Excuse me . . . er . . . small accident . . .

I . . . er . . . I go and sweep up . . .

You do that, old chap . . .

Ah, now for a nice pipe . . .

I'm sure I must have . . .

. . . some tobacco somewhere . . . . . .

Not in my jacket either . . . Thundering typhoons!

Ah, come to think of it . . . I must have left it on the plane . . . Confound it!

Never mind, I'll buy some more . . .

Hé, señor, where you go?

Me?

I'm out of tobacco: I'm going to buy some.

Tomorrow, señor.

You buy some tomorrow. Today, is too late!

Too late? . . . But it's barely eight o'clock!

Stop, señor! Return to your room!

?

Ten thousand thundering typhoons! You dare forbid me to go out? . . . Me, the guest of General Tapioca! . . .

Not go out, señor.

Señor not go out tonight! . . . Tomorrow . . . Too late tonight . . .

And why not, if you please? . . . Aren't I old enough to be out at night?

No, señor, but . . . er . . . Sometimes Picaros make attack around here . . . Is muy dangerous, señor . . . So you see, is best for your own protection . . .

Tomorrow, Excellency . . . tomorrow we bring tobacco for Your Excellency . . .

Certainly not! I want to buy my own tobacco!

As you wish, Excellency . . . Buenas noches, Excellency . . .

. . . 'night!

SLAM

That young whippersnapper Tintin was right, by thunder . . . The cage may be a gilded one . . .

. . . but we're well and truly behind bars!

Ah, there you are, Cap . . .

FLOP

When are you going to stop these childish pranks?

Next morning . . .

RAT TAT TAT

. . . MMM . . . yes . . . C'm in . . .

Buenos dias, Excellency . . . Your tobacco, Excellency . . .

My tobacco? . . . Tobacco? . . . What tobacco?

Tobacco you order last night, Excellency.

I told you I'd go and buy it myself, ten thousand thundering typhoons! . . . Myself, d'you hear?

Very good, Excellency. I go and get escort ready, Excellency . . .

What escort? An escort to go and buy tobacco?

Yes, Excellency, must have escort . . . Is necessary, because of terrorists, you understand: los Picaros . . .

WHOWOWOWOWOW

An hour later . . .

Ah, you're back. Would you believe that Tintin . . .

Tintin? He was jolly sensible to stay in Marlinspike!

He was absolutely right: we're prisoners, lock, stock and barrel!

I can see our hosts have a true sense of hospitality. That's what I just said to him . . .

. . . and he entirely agrees with me.

WHO agrees with you??? . . . And about WHAT???

Exactly, and what's more, he'll tell you so himself!

Won't you, my friend?

¡Buenos días, Captain!

Tintin, where in heaven's name have you sprung from?

Well, I've come straight from Marlinspike . . . You don't look very pleased to see me!

Why didn't you stay there, you silly fellow?

Let's say I was missing you, Captain . . .

. . . and the Professor too, of course.

On a horse? We came by car.

You'd hardly left when I began to blame myself for not having gone with you. I thought of all our friends in prison and the need to try to save them . . . So I took a plane . . . It's quite simple . . .

And it's crazy!

Because you were right! Would you believe . . .

Ssh!

Ah! You've got a record here I simply adore! . . . May I put it on, Captain?

AH! MY BEAUTY #

Have you gone raving mad?

?

Come, I want to show you something.

What?

There, look!

A microphone! The pirates!

And there's another! . . . The place is bugged, Captain!

And I'm pretty sure they'll have cameras hidden in every corner . . . I'd bet my life on it . . .

Behind a two-way mirror, for instance, like this one perhaps . . .

Aha! He's no fool, that boy!

No fool! He uses his head. But as I foresaw, that didn't stop him following the others into the trap I prepared for them . . .

A trap, Colonel?

A trap, yes . . . You see, before I was appointed by General Kûrvi-Tasch to be technical adviser to General Tapioca, I was Chief of Police in Szohôd, and those three . . .

. . . busybodies subjected me to a bitter humiliation!

You, Colonel, humiliated?

Yes, me . . .

. . . and I've never forgotten it . . . But fate sometimes plays into one's hands . . . When I heard that Bianca Castafiore was planning a tour in South America I immediately . . .

. . . realised how I could take advantage of the situation. I only had to arrest her, after forging compromising documents and having them slipped into her luggage . . . I concocted an entirely fictitious . . .

. . . conspiracy against General Tapioca . . . it only remained for me to give an international slant to the affair . . . And there it was . . . a brilliant conception, eh?

But WHEN are we going to see that confounded fellow Tapioca? After all, that's the principal reason we came here!

Instead of which, for three days they've shuttled us from the Museum of Ethnography to the birthplace of the Great Liberator, General Olivaro . . .

POP

. . . then to the zoo, then to the cathedral of the Santisima Virgen de la Inmaculada Concepcion . . . And what marvel have they in store for us tomorrow?

A confetti-maker for the carnival? . . . Or perhaps a sombrero factory? . . . Heaven knows what!

? + ? + ?

UGHHH!

Billions of blue blistering barnacles! What's happened to me? Why can't I take a single drop of alcohol any more?

RAT TAT TAT

Come in!

He! he!

RAT TAT TAT

YES! COME!

Buenas tardes, señores . . .

Hello, surely that isn't Manolo's voice?

The evening papers, señores . . .

PABLO!?!

Great snakes! . . . What a surprise! . . . I never . . .

Sssh!

Good evening, señores. My name is Pablo. I've been sent to replace Manolo, who suffered a slight accident this morning . . .

THAT?

Nothing serious, luckily: just a sprain.

YES? . . .

. . . He'll be back in a day or two.

OK!

Waste no time, amigos! Your lives are in danger!

Our lives?

In danger?

Yes. The day after tomorrow a commando of Picaros, but not real Picaros, will pretend to attack this villa. In the course of the fighting, quite by accident, all three of you will be killed!

What?

The official version: the Picaros tried to kidnap you!

But anyway, why all the palaver? . . . And who wants to kill us?

Do you know who runs the Security Police in this country? No? . . . Well, it's Colonel Esponja, or, to give him his real name: Sponsz.

Sponsz!!!

. . . Who was Chief of Police in Szohôd?

That's the one! He's been "lent" to General Tapioca to reorganise the Security Police in San Theodoros . . . and when he heard of Signora Castafiore's arrival, he dreamed up a plan to get rid of the three of you . . .

Luckily for you, the Picaros and their leader General Alcazar have eyes and ears everywhere . . . So this is what we're going to do. Tomorrow, Colonel Alvarez will take you on a trip to Hotuatabotl to see an ancient pyramid . . .

You'll climb to the top, with me. The soldiers will simply encircle the base. Then a commando of Picaros, real Picaros this time, will open fire on the northern face of the pyramid . . .

Ha! ha! ha! Success, success!

Under cover of the diversion you'll climb down the south face, having disarmed me and carefully tied me up. Two hundred metres away, right in front of you, one of Alcazar's trucks will be waiting . . .

Thanks, Pablo! Saving my life is becoming a habit with you. This is the second time!

Not far now: we're coming to the forest. We'll be there in a quarter of an hour . . .

Your young friend seems very preoccupied . . .

Oh, you've noticed it too?

He's upset to have had no word from General Tapioca.

So long as that's all it is! . . . I forgot to tell you, General Tapioca will see you tomorrow morning, and . . . Ah! there's the pyramid!

Magnificent, eh?

Superb! . . . Marvellous! . . . Can we go up?

Of course. But you'll excuse me if I don't accompany you . . .

I expect you've often climbed it before?

Very often. But Pablo will act as your guide.

They're all yours, Pablo.

Very good, Colonel.

Be careful. It's a steep slope and many people get giddy up there.

You are most thoughtful, Colonel.

Come along, Professor.

No thank you, Captain, I'd rather stay here. As you know, I suffer from vertigo . . .

No, no, you must come! There'll be a spectacular view from the top!

That's right, you go without me.

Cuthbert, come along, I beg of you! . . .

Great sunspots! I told you I don't want to!

Puma calling jaguar! . . . Puma calling jaguar! . . . Are you receiving me? . . . Come in now . . . Over . . .

Jaguar calling Puma! . . . Jaguar calling Puma! . . . Receiving you strength five . . . Over.

The truck's on its way . . . they'll be with you in seven or eight minutes . . . Mind you don't miss!

Be like missing an elephant at three metres in an alley, Colonel . . . And I've never done that yet!

You see, General Alcazar is true to his friends!

You can count on me! . . . So the minute I received your message I decided to move . . .

Our message? . . . You say you received a message from us?

Sure, the one Pablo brought me . . . What's the matter? You seem surprised about something.

I certainly am! . . . Because we never sent you any message . . . On the contrary, it was Pablo who told us, from you, that our lives were in danger but that you'd pull us out of trouble.

To me it stinks of treachery, General!

Treachery? . . . Impossible! . . . Pablo is dead loyal!

But Pablo lied to us, as he did to you . . . And with what object?

How should I know?

It bothers me, General . . . I've got a feeling someone's setting a trap for us . . .

Let's stop, General: we need time to think . . .

No way, amigo! We've a long trip ahead . . . and there's nothing to fear.

Jaguar calling Puma . . . We can see the truck now . . .

A direct hit? . . . Well done, Captain! . . . Are they all dead?

I've sent men to check, Colonel!

Colonel Esponja will be pleased with you, Pablo.

Jaguar calling Puma . . . Jaguar calling Puma . . .

Yes, I'm receiving you . . . What's that? . . . The truck's empty? . . . What?! . . . Because of the monkey . . . What monkey??? . . . Explain yourself, you imbecile!!!

No, they don't dare follow. They know we'll soon be in Arumbaya country . . . And that scares the living daylights out of them!

My other guerrillas who covered our escape while they pretended to attack will catch us up by another route . . . As for Pablo, that creep . . . Just wait till I get my hands on Pablo!

The dirty rat! I'll have him eaten alive by red ants!

I must admit I never suspected him for a moment . . .

A charming walk, isn't it, Captain?

Charming: you've said it! . . . To think we could be home at good old Marlinspike, downing a cool glass of beer!

But Captain, I ask you: why did you make me climb to the top of that pyramid and then rush me straight down the other side? . . . You must admit it's very odd . . .

Mmm . . .

I'm not really cross with you because the view certainly was spectacular.

There on the ground! . . . Columbus! Am I dreaming?

"Loch Lomond"?

Here, in a tropical forest? . . . Unbelievable!

Stop! Don't drink that!

!

I was only going to taste it . . .

They all say that . . . and swig the lot!

There!

Oh!

Wooah!

The next thing is a splitting headache!

A headache? . . . From "Loch Lomond"? . . . Never!

BONG

Over there . . .

I can't believe it! . . .

?

Wooah!

Look: a parachute!

Another present from that hoodlum Tapioca! . . . He's trying to neutralise the Arumbayas and my Picaros at the same time by dropping cases of whisky by parachute . . . You've seen the result: even the monkeys have taken to the bottle!

ICEBERG DEAD AHEAD!

?

!

Hard a' starboard!

That crack on the head must have done it!

Look, Captain . . .

Who's captain here, you or me?

You, of course; you're Captain Haddock . . .

How ridiculous! . . . What's my first name, then?

Archibald, isn't it?

Even worse! . . . What's yours?

My name's Tintin.

Grotesque!

To crown it all, I've lost my ship . . . Perhaps it's flown away.

Look, Captain, ships don't fly!

Oh no? . . . That's what you think . . . Mine does! It's an airship, so there!

!Come on, vamos! We must reach the Arumbaya village before dark.

We'll stop and spend the night there . . . Have a cigar, amigo?

No, thanks.

. . . We'll move on again at dawn.

. . . As I said before, you will note that I am not reproaching you, for the view really was very fine from the summit of the pyramid, but . . .

As Napoleon said, "Think of it, soldiers, forty centuries look down upon you."

No, no, we're good pals with the Arumbayas. To begin with they gave us a load of trouble. But now there isn't any danger . . .

POF POF POF

THACK

Ridgewell! . . . You never get any better do you, you old joker! . . . Come on out of there!

Hello, General! . . . Hello, Tintin! . . . It's good to see you again!

Nice to be back, Doctor Ridgewell! . . . How are the Arumbayas? . . . Learnt to play golf yet?

Don't talk about it! . . . But on the other hand they've made great strides . . . in drunkenness, I'm afraid . . . By courtesy of General Tapioca!

LET ME GO! . . . TINTIN!!! . . . HELP!!! . . .

Tintin, help! . . . Save me! . . . Stop thief! . . . Fire! . . . Police! . . . Help, I am undone!

Ha! ha! ha!

Wotat it'fa!

Ha! ha! ha!

That's enough! . . . Gi'dahda vit!

You see? . . . Tapioca has a lot to answer for . . . Come, we must go. The village is still some distance away.

Dipsomaniacs! . . . That's what "civilisation" has done for those "savages".

That evening . . .

There's the Arumbaya village.

Excuse me, Captain . . . I see they are preparing some sort of meal over there . . .

He! he! . . .

OOH!!! ? ?

? ?

♪ ♪ ♪

Avakuki, chief of the Arumbayas, has invited us to share their meal . . . and to spend the night in his own hut.

Please thank him from us and tell him we accept with pleasure. Don't we, Captain?

Full astern!

Don't we, Professor ? . . . ? . . . ?

Oh! Now where's he got to? . . .

Ah, I see. There he is . . . just coming along behind . . .

That evening . . .

You may not fancy this very much, but pretend to like it: it's important not to offend them . . .

Don't worry . . .

Bon appetit, Professor!

Certainly not. On the contrary, I'm passionately fond of all exotic foods!

Owzah g'rubai?

He's asking if you like it.

It's absolutely stunning!

Isn't it, Professor?

HHHH!

Oozfa sek 'unds?

He says you must have some more. And he's right: their "otnōsh" is particularly highly seasoned today.

I . . . I know!

Ava'n ip?

It's time for the toasts now. You must drink it straight down at one gulp . . .

Goes without saying!

Your very good health, mighty chief Avakuki!

Come on, make an effort . . .

? !

PFOUAGH!

Young idiot! D'you want to get yourself murdered?

I'm . . . I'm terribly sorry . . . I couldn't swallow it . . . That whisky's simply disgusting!

Disgusting?!!! When you travel, you try to respect local customs! . . . Otherwise, you stay at home!

I'm terribly sorry, but I simply couldn't . . . It's too nasty . . .

PFOUAGH!

Goh'blimeh! Wa'samma ta, li li li va? . . . Lem eshohya!

Sum in'ksup wivit!

GLUG GLUG GLUG

Well I never! That's the first time it hasn't worked!

! ?

WAOAOOAOW!

He! he!

WA AAAAH!

". . . it seems that he too has temporarily given up whisky . . ."

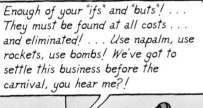

The next morning . . .

Poor Captain, he doesn't seem any better . . .

Meanwhile . . .

. . . and our helicopters resumed their search this morning. But they have a difficult assignment as you will understand. Because of the forest terrain, the fugitives will be well hidden. If, on the other hand . . .

Enough of your "ifs" and "buts"! . . . They must be found at all costs . . . and eliminated! . . . Use napalm, use rockets, use bombs! We've got to settle this business before the carnival, you hear me?!

RRRRRRRRR

A helicopter! . . . But there isn't any danger so long as we remain under cover.

RRRRRRRR

Hey, Captain! Stop!

RRRRRRRR

Stop! . . . Captain, take cover!

A man . . . at three o'clock!

RRRRRRR

Captain! Stop!!!

SPLOSH

Hello . . . That's odd . . . I can't see anyone now . . . Yet I'm positive I saw . . .

OK, don't worry . . . We'll make another pass . . .

Well, where's your chap, eh?

FLOUFLOUFLOUFLOUFLOUF

GLUB

GLUB

There . . . You satisfied now?

Quick! . . . Get him out!

Still, I could have sworn I saw something move.

All right, we'll try again . . .

Oh no! They're coming back!

Sorry, Captain!

GLUG

?

FLOUFLOUFLOUFLOUF

GLUB

GLUB

That satisfy you . . . Convinced this time?

Mmmm . . .

Whew! . . . Saved!

You probably saw a cayman . . .

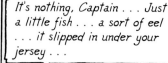

It's nothing, Captain . . . Just a little fish . . . a sort of eel . . . it slipped in under your jersey . . .

WOW! OW! OWW!

Yes, it's a gymnotus . . . a dear little gymnotus: an electric fish . . .

Lucky for you it was only a little one. Big electric eels grow up to a couple of metres long and can stun a horse with a single discharge!

Well, lucky for me that I'm not a horse!

Ah, I see what it is . . .

I'll put it back in the water . . .

There!

Come, señores, it's time we were moving on. It's a long way from here to the camp and we do better to get there in daylight . . .

That evening . . .

Nearly there . . . Just another quarter of an hour, and we'll be with my Picaros.

Are there a lot of Picaros?

Oh, at least thirty . . .

And you plan to regain power with thirty men? . . . I must say, General, you certainly have plenty of nerve.

Sure, hombre! It's perfectly possible, but only during the carnival. For those three days the hooch flows like water . . . even the garrison get hopelessly drunk . . . So, if we want to succeed, we have to mount our operation during the carnival.

BANG   BANG

RATATATATAT

¡BASTA!

¡Caramba, caballeros! . . . ¡El general!

¿El general?

¡Ah, si, el general! . . . ¡Viva el general!

¿Qué, el general?

¡Buenosh diash 'eneral! . . . We wondered . . . hic . . . what'd happened . . . hic . . . t'ya! . . .

Shi! . . . we were . . . hic . . . muy anshush . . .

Thass why we . . . hic . . . hadda li'l drink!

Shi! . . . To forget . . . hic that we were . . . hic . . . anshush!

But now that you've come, we aren't anshush any more . . .

Asholutely not!

Sho we'll have a li'l drink to shelebrate, won't we, amigosh? . . .

HIPS

Enough! Touch another drop and I'll shoot!

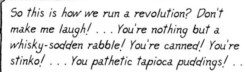

So this is how we run a revolution? Don't make me laugh! . . . You're nothing but a whisky-sodden rabble! You're canned! You're stinko! . . . You pathetic tapioca puddings! . . .

HIC   HIPS

Get to your quarters this instant! . . . Parade in fifteen minutes in full combat kit! . . . Dismiss!!

HIPS

HIC

You see?

Sadly, yes . . .

Tapioca succeeded all too well with his parachute drops of whisky! . . . ¡Caramba! How can one mount a revolution with that bunch of drunks?

Alcazar! . . . So you decided to come back at last, did you?

¡AY!

40

Look who's here! . . . And just where d'you think ___ you've been, Mr Big?

Good-evening, Peggy, my dove!

You promised me to be home the same night! . . . And you've been gone three whole days!

I can explain, palomita mia . . .

Yeah, yeah, I know: any excuse is better than none! And what about me, left to rot in a lousy mud hut? . . . That's real dandy!

The General promised me a palace in Tapiocapolis! And all the General provides is a beat-up palliasse crawling with bugs and roaches!

But . . .

These guys your friends? . . . OK, I warn them: they think they're gonna make the rules around here, they're mighty mistaken!

Thank you, gracious lady, for those kind words! . . . Please believe that we are extremely touched by your generous welcome, and allow me to offer you our most humble respects . . .

SMACK

That a weak woman should share the hardships and, let us admit it, the dangers of guerrilla life, commands not only our utmost respect but our profound admiration!

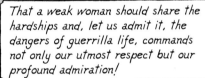

. . . And I speak in all sincerity, dear lady!

You coming, Alcazar?

Yes, my dove.

She seems a little . . . er . . . brisk . . . on first acquaintance, but she has a heart of gold . . .

Of course, General. One sees it immediately . . .

What a delightful lady! . . . So graceful . . . Such exquisite femininity! . . . As for that poor man . . .

. . . his revolution will never succeed with a collection of drunkards like that . . . Never, unless someone gives him a hand . . . And it is I who will do it . . . I, Cuthbert Calculus!

You?

You'll . . . ?

No, gentlemen, I am not a fool! I know exactly what I am saying!

You've missed a . . .

My sister??? . . . What about my sister? . . . What's my sister done to you? . . . Will you be good enough to leave my sister out of this? . . . And now, listen to me . . .

I . . .

Yes . . .

You see this tube of tablets? Well, it contains a product that I have recently perfected. It has a base of medicinal herbs . . .

The preparation has no taste, no smell, and is absolutely non-toxic. Having said that, a single one of these tablets administered in either food or drink imparts a disgusting taste to any alcohol taken thereafter . . .

. . . And the very first person upon whom I tested it was you, Captain!

ME?

You dared to do that? . . . Borgia! . . . Cannibal! . . . Miserable blundering barbecued blister . . .

I tell you my sister has absolutely nothing to do with it!

And furthermore, you can thank me for being concerned for your health!

Please, Captain!

It's a disgrace! . . . A scandal! . . . A monstrous attack upon the personal freedom of the individual!

Precisely! . . . And again yesterday, with the Indians, you could see for yourselves the efficacy of my invention . . .

But I never knew you had . . .

No, young man, I am not mad! . . . And I would ask you to show a little more respect towards a man of mature years!

No, no, I insist . . . er . . .

And for heaven's sake stop talking about my sister!

My sister . . . just a moment . . . My sister???

. . . And another thing! . . . I don't have a sister . . . I never had a sister . . . And don't you forget it!

So there!

A revolution without executions? . . . Without reprisals? . . . ¡Caramba! . . . It's unthinkable! . . . You must be joking! . . . And anyway, what about tradition? . . . Yes, what about tradition, eh? Answer me that!

No, what you ask is impossible, amigo . . . Tapioca and his ministers are bloody tyrants and villains . . .

They must be shot! . . . Every man jack of them! . . . Shot, d'you hear me?

Very well, General.

We won't discuss it further . . . And forgive me for bothering you . . .

Hey! but . . . Wait . . . Perhaps we . . .

Goodbye, General.

?

BOOM

What have you done? . . .

Ha! ha! ha! Funny joke! A teeny tear-gas grenade!

Who did that? . . . I'll have him shot!

One of your Picaros. Blind drunk, as usual . . .

Hmm! . . . Not easy to mount a successful revolution with that bunch of boozers, is it, General?

All right, you win! I accept your proposition!

You do?

But at least you'll let me shoot Tapioca and his ministers? . . . And his staff officers? . . . You wouldn't refuse me that?

You won't shoot anyone, General!

No one but Tapioca and his ministers, then . . .

I said no one! You can take it or leave it!

But it's mean! You're taking advantage of the situation! . . . D'you realise I'll be nothing but a figure of fun if I do as you say?

GRRR

At least let me shoot Tapioca! . . . Just Tapioca, I implore you!

No.

I'll cure your Picaros of their drunkenness, and you'll promise me not to use any violence while I'm helping you to regain power . . . Agreed? . . . All right, say after me: I promise!

I promise . . .

Good, I have your word . . . For my part, I promise that soon your Picaros won't touch a drop more alcohol.

Good! . . . But just you watch your step! If you've given me false hope . . . you'll be up against a wall, pronto! Understand?

Y . . . yes!

Ah, hello!

?

Has he lost something?

Yes, he must have lost something . . .

You seem to have lost something . . .

No, no, I've lost something . . .

The bottle of tablets I was telling you about just now . . . I can't find it anywhere . . . Isn't that curious?

Hey, you seem very upset that he's lost the tablets?

I'll say I am! I promised the General his Picaros would soon stop drinking!

You promised that?

Yes, it's obvious . . . if his men go on boozing, he won't ever get his revolution!

Well? We don't give a tinker's cuss for his revolution, anyway!

Yes, Captain, we certainly do . . .

. . . because our friends the Thompsons, Signora Castafiore, Irma and Mr Wagner are in danger . . . And the only way to save them is for Alcazar to defeat Tapioca and take over the government!

You're right, by thunder!

Oh, very well, here's his rotten old bottle! I pinched it from him, to stop him curing people of their pleasures!

?

Be a good fellow: give it back to him yourself. He'll be so grateful to you . . .

If you insist . . .

Is this what you're looking for, by any chance?

!

Captain, you're an angel!

SMACK

Thanks to you, those poor creatures will be delivered from their passion for alcohol at last! . . . Like you, Captain!

Tintin! . . . Tintin! . . .

That's the General!

Come quick, amigo! . . . The trial of your friends . . . it's on television!

!

Television? . . . Here? . . . They must have a portable generator.

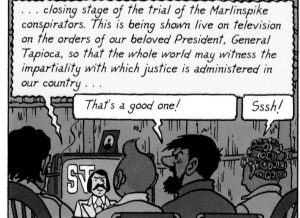

. . . closing stage of the trial of the Marlinspike conspirators. This is being shown live on television on the orders of our beloved President, General Tapioca, so that the whole world may witness the impartiality with which justice is administered in our country . . .

That's a good one!

Sssh!

Recently, our beloved President generously invited Captain Haddock, Professor Calculus and the reporter Tintin to our country to put their case. He guaranteed their freedom. And how did they repay him? With cold cynicism! They took the first opportunity to flee into the jungle and join their accomplice Alcazar and his villainous Picaros!

This action alone is enough to prove that the grave accusations against the three defendants are entirely justified. But over now to the Palace of Justice where the Public Prosecutor is putting the case for the Republic . . .

. . . You have before you, gentlemen, two sinister characters who, more easily to accomplish their evil purpose . . . Do I need to remind you of it? . . .

. . . to assassinate our beloved President . . . did not hesitate to pass themselves off as honest policemen! . . . But their monstrous subterfuge deceived no one! Look at their low brows, their furtive glances!

. . . In short, look at their brutish faces! Policemen? Them? . . . Cheats! Imposters! Assassins!

. . . Men who, to appear as loyal supporters of General Tapioca and the noble ideology of Kûrvi-Tasch, carried their duplicity so far as to grow moustaches!

That's a lie! . . . We've been wearing moustaches since we were born!

To be precise: we're worn bearing them!

Silence! . . . You will speak when you are spoken to!

. . . Gentlemen, for these two wretches, who can have no claim to extenuating circumstances, I demand the DEATH PENALTY!

You see? None of your fancy scruples there, eh?

The death penalty!! . . . He certainly doesn't mince his words . . . He means to go the whole hog!

To be precise: his words certainly mean he's going to mince the hog whole!

But the real brains behind the plot . . . and we have here documents which prove it irrefutably . . . are those of a woman!!!

A woman . . . or should we call her a monster? . . . who lent her talents, her undoubted talents to a criminal cause: her name is Bianca Castafiore, "the Milanese Nightingale"!

Help! ... Help! ... Save me!

The Professor!

Kill the traitor!

Hang him!

He's a traitor, General ... a saboteur! ... We caught him red handed, just as he was emptying a bottle of pills into the cooking pot!

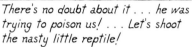

There's no doubt about it ... he was trying to poison us! ... Let's shoot the nasty little reptile!

General?

Yes?

.........?

......!

..........!!

!

No need to panic, boys! This man is a good friend of the Picaros: I can vouch for him. He isn't trying to poison you ... quite the opposite. He's giving you Vitamin C ... What for? ... Quite simply, to make you strong ... to beat the daylights out of that loathesome Tapioca!

Are you sure?

Ah! well ...

Sure as I stand here! ... Eat away! ... I give you my solemn word ... you won't come to any harm!

I'm sorry, Professor? ... Are you all right?

Take all night? ... Not nearly as long ... In a couple of hours at most my pills will take effect ...

From that moment, none of those men will be able to stomach a single drop of alcohol! ... Just like you, Captain! ... Isn't that marvellous?

GNNNN!

¡Gracias, hombre, gracias!

MBLL ...

And to show my appreciation, I create you companion of the order of San Fernando, first class!

A glass? ... How nice! ... A little iced water will be delicious ...

Whatever the General may say, I'm not eating that stuff ...

These new-fangled chemicals ... you never can tell ...

Look at them, Captain . . . They're obviously suspicious . . . And if they don't eat that food they'll go on drinking . . . So the revolution will fail . . . and our friends the Thompsons will be shot!

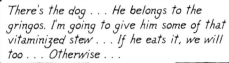

There's the dog . . . He belongs to the gringos. I'm going to give him some of that vitaminized stew . . . If he eats it, we will too . . . Otherwise . . .

He's right!

I agree!

Doggy woggy? . . . Come come come come . . .

Hello, what does he want me for?

Come come come! . . . Yummy yum! . . . Looky dere! . . . Looky dere, good for little dogsywogsies! . . .

He must be daft, talking like that . . .

Let's hope . . . let's hope he'll eat the food . . .

SNIFF SNIFF SNIFF

?

YEEEK!

You saw that, boys? . . . Are we going to eat what even a dog won't touch?

You're right!

We won't eat that muck!

Go back at once, Snowy, and eat it!

But . . .

That slop! It's full of pimentos!

SCHLOOP SLURP GLUP SCHLOP

Hey, boys! Look! . . . He's changed his mind! . . . Now we can have some too!

¡Bueno! I'm hungry!

They're eating it! Now we can save our friends!

TOOT

! ?

Hello, a b-b-b- . . . hic . . . bus!

Ah! Not a pink elephant today, then?

Is it far to Tapiocapolis, chum?

Tapiocapolis? . . . Great snakes, you're hopelessly off the road.

Drat! . . . Could any of these soldiers escort us? . . . I've heard there's a risk of attack from guerrillas around here . . . they call them Picaros.

That's exactly where you are: among the Picaros!

No kidding?

Are these real guerrillas?

It's terrifically Tarzan, dear, don't you think?

I say, old man, where can we buy postcards?

Poshe . . . hic . . . cardsh?

They must have a souvenir shop somewhere about the place . . .

Blow me, look who's here!

Jolyon Wagg!

Doctor Livingstone, I presume! How are you, me old salt? On holiday?

No!

Don't tell me, you laid it on as a surprise! You're part of the welcome to the carnival! It's going to be a wow this year: thanks to us!

Thanks to you?

Bet your life! . . . Know the charity concert party, The Jolly Follies? . . . That's us! . . . And guess who's leader of the band: yours truly!

Ah! er...

Sunny Jim designed their costumes, too . . . Smashing, eh?

Very . . . original!

What's all this tomfoolery?

Who's that?

General Alcazar, leader of the Picaros.

Hi there, me old Field Marshal! ... So you're the top brass for these boozy brigands!

What d'you think you're doing here, you and your busload of ballerinas? ... And come to think of it, for all I know you're spies on Tapioca's payroll!

A word with you, General, if I may ...

. . . . ? . . . .
. . . . ??? . . . .
. . . . . ? . . . . ??
. . . . ???. .

✿☆✧ "✧ ⚙ ✉ ..☆.
CLAC...TR2TRRRR...
RR...TING ½ CLANG
$\frac{m}{c}$ 2 ▥ ◎ ..CLICK?
✿ × 3.1416 !!!!

CLICK

Tintin, amigo mio, you're a genius! ... A real genius! ... I shall admit you to the Order of San Fernando!

Thanks, General.

Welcome to the Picaros,   señor.

Please forgive me, amigo mio: I didn't realise who you were! ... But caramba! Friends of my friends are friends of mine! So make yourself at home, hombre!

And this evening, amigo, you and all your Follies will be my guests! Si, si! We'll have a grand fiesta, with whisky by the gallon! Just you wait!

What did you say to him?

You'll see in due course!

¡Caramba! These Jolly Follies were sent from heaven! . . . Thanks to them and to your friend Calculus I'll soon be back in power . . .

It's a shabby way to treat those poor people, sneaking off with their bus and their costumes. But it's the only way to save our friends . . .

Never mind, I'll be able to reward them with appropriate generosity as soon as I've chucked out that vile Tapioca: I'll admit them all to the Order of San Fernando!

Tomorrow afternoon we'll arrive in Tapiocapolis . . . and that'll soon be renamed Alcazaropolis. It's the opening day of the carnival. Before we reach the city we'll rehearse our plans to the very last detail . . .

We'll be dressed in the Jolly Follies costumes, with our guns at the ready . . .

With orders not to use them!

The next afternoon . . .

This is it, my brave Picaros! We're here! . . . Now each of you guys: remember what you have to do . . .

VIVA TAPIOCA

COURTESY OF LOCH LOMOND

CALLE 22 DE MAYO

CONDENADO A LA MUERTE

Meanwhile . . .

Are you sure it isn't dangerous, General, letting all these people assemble in front of the windows? You'll be a sitting target for the first Picaro . . .

No danger, Colonel . . .

. . . Even if by some extraordinary chance armed Picaros managed to infiltrate the crowd, they'd be far too drunk to shoot straight! . . . As you know, my parachute drops of whisky have been a total success.

My spies have been quite definite: Alcazar's men are never sober . . . And they'd be quite incapable of engaging in any serious action, poor fools . . .

This is it, boys!

Everybody out!

Watch it, Captain, remember you're a Folly!

Don't worry!

♪ WE'RE THE ♪ JOLLY JOLLY FOLLIES . . . ♩ HEY NONNY NO . . . ♪ HEY NONNY NO . . . . 🎵

Where are those people from?

The programme says: "The Jolly Follies, a charity concert party from Europe".

Excellent! . . . Just listen to the beat! . . . They've even got our guards joining in the dance!

Ready! . . . On the next hey nonny no, out comes the chloroform!

HEY NONNY NO! ?

Put him with the rest in the porch. Your guns are there . . .

55

Ha! ha! ha! They're hilarious! Have some of them brought up here. I'd like to meet these jolly fellows!

As the General wishes!

You sent for us, General? Here we are! . . . Happy carnival!

? ! ?

What sort of joke is this?

It isn't a joke, my dear Tapioca. Look who's here!

ALCAZAR!!!

GENERAL Alcazar to you, EX-General Tapioca!

Look, Captain. D'you recognise that officer there, next to Colonel Alvarez?

Thundering typhoons! Sponsz!

Now, my dear Tapioca, you will kindly read out this little speech prepared by us. We shall, of course, be recording it on tape . . .

I will never read it!

Tut tut! . . . Never say never, amigo!

Very well, I surrender to violence, but I protest!

Get on with it! And make it sound convincing!

Friends, comrades, countrymen! . . . This carnival day marks a turning-point in the history of our native land . . .

. . . For today I have decided to hand over all my powers to General Alcazar, who, from now on, will lead our beloved country forward along the road of economic, social and cultural progress! . . . Long live San Theodoros! . . . Long live General Alcazar!

Thanks, amigo! You'll be a sensation on the radio!

There it is . . . in the bag! . . . Pedro, you and your section hop along to the Radio Building and see this statement is broadcast immediately . . . Understand?

Si!

My heartiest congratulations, General! . . . Death to Tapioca! . . . Would you like him shot at once?

Long live General Alcazar!

Shoot Tapioca!

Long live General Alcazar!

Executions are out! . . . His life will be spared.

But General, it's contrary to every custom . . . The people will be terribly disappointed . . .

The Colonel is right, General . . . For pity's sake don't pardon me! Do you want me completely dishonoured?

Permit me to insist, General!

My decision is irrevocable: your life will be spared! An aircraft will be placed at your disposal, to convey you wherever you may wish to go.

Are you mad?

No, I'm not . . . But he is! . . . This muchacho made me give my word that the coup would be bloodless! . . . I'm desperately sorry . . .

Come on, let's greet old Sponsz . . .

Ah, an idealist, is he? . . . Young chaps nowadays have absolutely no respect for anything . . . Not even the oldest traditions!

We live in sad times!

We meet again, Colonel Sponsz!

!

Don't worry, Sponsz, even you have nothing to fear. They're pining for you in Borduria, so your ticket to Szohôd is booked for the morning . . .

We caught this joker trying to escape . . .

It's Tintin! . . . I'm finished!

Pablo!

Mercy, Señor Tintin, mercy! Please don't shoot me!

That's less than you deserve, you subtropical sea-louse!

Don't be afraid, Pablo; no one is going to hurt you. You once saved my life, and I haven't forgotten that . . . You are free to go . . . Adios, Pablo!

You made a mistake there, Tintin, and you'll live to regret it. You're making a rod for your own back . . . To be precise . . .

Great snakes! The Thompsons!

The Thompsons, General! . . . The Thompsons! . . . They could be shot while we stand here talking!

Ah, yes . . . you think so?

Yes, General. The execution is due to take place in twenty-two minutes, precisely!

¡Mil bombas! Quick, call the prison and cancel the execution!

At once, General!

RRING
· · · · ·
RRING

. . . fifty seconds . . . Pip Pip Pip . . . At the third stroke it will be five thirty-eight precisely . . . Pip Pip Pip . . . At the third . . .

You did it on purpose! Dial the right number this time, or I'll have you shot!

RRRRRING
· · · · · · ·
RRRRRING

. . . precisely . . . Pip Pip Pip . . . At the third stroke it will be five forty and ten seconds.

If it doesn't work this time, I'll personally shoot the Minister of Telecommunications!!

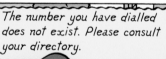

The number you have dialled does not exist. Please consult your directory.

Only one thing to do: dash to the prison and save them ourselves!

Take B Section with you! The Colonel will guide you! I'll have his head if you're too late!

¡Rápido! . . . ¡Rápido . . . por Dios!

Meanwhile . . .

I'm terribly sorry, gentlemen, but we must go, please . . . It's time . . .

And one must be on time.

To be precise: time, gentlemen please!

Don't worry: it's a nasty moment, but you'll soon forget it . . .

This is San Theodoros National Radio. We are interrupting our programmes for a special announcement by His Excellency General Tapioca . . .

A car! . . . We must commandeer a car!

Useless! No vehicle could get through this crowd . . .

What can we do?

Look! That float . . .

What? You mean . . .

Yes! It's the only possible answer!

You! . . . Keep on playing!

Keep playing! . . . Don't stop!

Driver! . . . To the State Prison! And put your foot down!

Put my foot down? . . . With this crate? . . . You must be joking!

TOOOT VROOM

TOOT

Blindfolds? Certainly not! . . . A Thompson looks death straight in the face!

To be precise: A Thomson with a straight face looks like death!

It's your lucky day. The music adds a little gaiety to the   party, doesn't it?

We simply must be in time!

Squ-a-a-a-d! . . . Ready!

Can you perhaps think of some famous last words?

Er . . . What about, "Kiss me, Thompson" . . . Will that do?

Squad! Take aim! . . .

Hold your fire! . . . Hands up, the lot of you! . . . Drop your guns!

? ?

Next morning . . .

The army, the navy and the air force have come over to me! ¡Mil bombas! It's an overwhelming triumph!

And it's partly due, of course, to you . . . Si, si, si! . . . Alcazar is not ungenerous: you will be decorated with the order of San Fernando! . . . As for your five per cent . . .

Please forget that, General!

General, the bus you sent to the camp to fetch Señora Alcazar and the Jolly Follies has returned.

Good! Show them in here . . .

So there you are, Alcazar! What's the game, eh? You've been absent without leave again!

I can explain, palomita mia . . .

Señor Wagg, allow me to express the deep gratitude of the San Theodorian people for the help you have given to our cause. I therefore appoint you and your Jolly Follies to the order of San Fernando, and invite you to next year's carnival.

And Señor Professor . . . In recognition of the magnificent role you played, I appoint you Knight Grand Cross of the Order of San Fernando, with Oak Leaves.

No thank you, my friend. Never between meals.

Good old Alcazar! Give him a big hurrah!

As for you, my dove . . . I promised you a palace. Bueno, I keep my word. This is all yours, from now on.

Fine and dandy! . . . Anyone can see it isn't you who's expected to keep this dump clean . . . So for a start, stop dropping cigar ash all over the place! . . . You get me?

Two days later . . .

Blistering barnacles, I shan't be sorry to be back home in Marlinspike . . .

Me too, Captain . . .

Me too, but with a little mustard   if you please.

VIVA ALCAZAR

THE END